Lightning Strike to the Heart

a Delta Force romance story

by

M. L. Buchman

D1495263

Copyright 2016 Matthew Lieber Buchman
Published by Buchman Bookworks

All rights reserved.
This book, or parts thereof,
may not be reproduced in any form
without permission from the author.
Discover more by this author at:
www.mlbuchman.com

Cover images:
Lightning Storm Cloud
© Positiveflash | Dreamstime
Young Man © Rvs | Dreamstime

Buchman Bookworks

Other works by M.L. Buchman

1

It was a bitter New Year's Eve, especially at thirty-three thousand feet standing on the open rear ramp of a C-130 Hercules cargo plane. The rain drummed on the plane's skin with such ferocity that she could barely hear the roar of the massive turboprop engines over the storm. She had to stay light on her toes to keep her balance on the shifting deck.

Chief Petty Officer Teresa Mann of the US Coast Guard checked her watch: oh-two hundred. Happy New Year. What better time, place, and weather for her first combat jump with a Delta. She'd been thrilled at the chance to accompany a Unit operator—as Delta Force soldiers called themselves—but this was a little extreme even by the Airborne Jumpmaster Course's harsh standards.

She'd done HALO jumps before—bail out at high-altitude but wait for the last second before doing a low opening—but not in the middle of the night during a major storm.

The C-130's Loadmaster spoke over the intercom wired into her earphones, "Jump in fifteen seconds." Only the dull red jumplight lit the cavernous rear of the aircraft. He and his assistant were anonymous in a full helmet and armored vest as the four of them grouped together for their final checks.

Teresa began counting backwards.

"Ground reports winds out of the southwest at forty," he provided the last key element before the jump.

In other words a total nightmare for the landing.

"In ten!" He was a second fast. Then he yanked her and the sergeant's communications cables, and her earphones went quiet.

He disconnected their oxygen hookups to the aircraft's supply system.

For a jump from this altitude, she and Hal were wearing full facemasks and carrying five minutes of oxygen. Instead of helmets, they wore insulated caps that fitted tightly against the mask. Five minutes allowed plenty of margin for error as they should fall into breathable air within ninety seconds, but they couldn't risk cracking their masks for the full three minutes of the jump until they deployed their chutes—the chance of getting frostbite from the wind chill was too high. They'd already checked each other head to toe to make sure there was no exposed skin. With a sixty-second margin of air, they were good to go.

The Loadmaster unlatched Master Sergeant Waldman and then her own safety lines that had kept them securely connected to the racing cargo plane once the rear ramp had been lowered.

Then the Loadmaster caressed her ass and gave it a hard squeeze.

Rather than going for the most obvious response—a sharp kick to the balls, which he was already turning aside to protect against in addition to having an armored flap dangling over his groin from his bullet-proof vest—she made her hand into a knife edge and drove her fingertips upward into his armpit through the gap in his armor between vest and sleeve. Once there, she grabbed and twisted the leading edge of the pectoral muscle hard enough that his arm wouldn't work right for days without causing a shooting pain down its whole length. She gave an extra yank; he'd walk with a hunch for most of that time.

His hand, which had clutched her even harder in initial shock, finally let go.

As he jerked it back, she brought the edge of her hand down in a hard chop that may or may not have broken his wrist.

By the volume of his scream—which was loud enough to be heard over the roar of rain and engine, despite no longer sharing the intercom—she'd guess a bad break. Hardly a traditional start to the New Year.

She stepped to the rear edge of the cargo ramp with Hal. At the last second Teresa turned so that she was facing the still screaming Loadmaster and his assistant, who was clawing at his headphone's volume control. She snapped to full attention as she stepped off the end of the ramp. With a sharp salute, she drifted off the plane and fell backwards into the storm.

"Any problems?" Hal asked over their short-range encrypted radio link as they slammed from the plane's two hundred miles an hour into freefall. Once they were flying with the wind, the battering eased.

"It depends Waldman, are you a macho asshole?" In the pitch dark, Teresa oriented herself head down and lined up her body for the fastest descent speed.

"I've been accused of the macho often enough. I try to avoid giving women a cause to call me an asshole though."

"Then we're fine."

2

Hal did his best to keep any thoughts about Chief Petty Officer Teresa Mann's fineness to himself as they plummeted downward through thirty thousand feet and headed toward twenty-five. By that time they had reached terminal velocity. At a hundred-and-fifty miles per hour, the rain wasn't merely noisy, it was also painful as it drove against his jumpsuit like a rapid fire BB gun.

There was no sign of the city that lay below; the clouds had gathered so thickly that no hint of light made it up to their altitude.

He'd seen the Loadmaster's grope and,

while he agreed that Mann had one of the best asses he'd ever seen in the military, he'd been trying to figure out how to report the man for his action as there wasn't either time or opportunity for him to step in and thrash the man himself without missing the jump window.

Then Mann had taken action of her own and absolved him from that part of the problem.

The primary difficulty with making a report was that the C-130's crew had been purposely misled to think that he and Teresa were a couple of crazy CIA spooks being sent in on some intelligence-gathering mission. So no one had asked anyone else's names and no units were mentioned. He and Mann had showed up at the designated place, found the aforementioned aircraft, and climbed aboard without a word.

Sending punishment meant reporting aspects of their mission to sections of the command authority that weren't supposed to know about its existence.

He had to admire the efficiency with which Mann had transferred the burden of explanation onto the Air Force Loadmaster. Now it would be up to him to explain how he'd broken his wrist and couldn't use his right arm properly without saying anything about how it had happened. And if he did talk about the two strangers who had jumped out of his aircraft, he'd be grounded so fast that he'd have to sprint to keep ahead of the dishonorable discharge that would be racing to catch up with him. The authority structure of Joint Special Operations Command wasn't a big fan of soldiers who violated their security clearances.

Despite being Coast Guard, Teresa Mann had used Unit thinking which was still disorienting. Rumor said that the first woman of Delta was out in the field and that another was in the Operators Training Course—even if neither possibility sounded very likely. Petty Officer Teresa Mann was on loan from the U.S. Coast Guard's MSST team—the USCG's special forces. If the anti-terrorist Maritime Safety and Security Team produced any other women as obviously skilled as Mann, he'd be seriously impressed. If they had any more that looked like her, he'd change branches of the service just for the female scenery.

He pulled his arm forward, keeping it close to his body to avoid invoking a mid-air tumble, to check the GPS and altimeter. Twenty thousand feet flashed by and he corrected his flight path ten degrees toward the southwest by briefly bending one knee to raise a foot into the wind. The rain pounded so hard against his plastic facemask that he couldn't have heard her if Mann was speaking, but they were in communication blackout anyway, so it shouldn't matter.

They fell through thick clouds, and despite their suits the wet and the wind chill were severe enough that he'd be shivering if the jump adrenaline wasn't pumping so hard. A bolt of lightning slashed somewhere nearby and for a second he saw Mann in clear outline just a hundred feet away, dressed in pitch black against a background of heavy storm, cloud-lit brilliantly from within. Then they were plunged back into darkness.

It was a glimpse he knew he'd never forget, Teresa Mann as Wonder Woman—no, Catwoman—dressed all in black, flying fearlessly through the storm, and dangerous as hell. He thanked whatever Army god had kicked the extraction assignment in his direction just forty-eight hours ago.

HALO jump to listed coordinates. Escort individual to safety. Zero profile.

Which in Delta-speak meant: "don't be seen, even if you have to kill someone—but don't do that either." He considered possible scenarios based on the limited information. Command would have provided more if they had it, which meant he was jumping into an unknown situation, expected to carry out a barely defined mission, and not to be caught. That's why the mission had come to Delta—no one rocked the unknown like The Unit.

But the best option for keeping low cover on the ground would be a man-woman team, so he'd sent a request up the command chain without much hope. But for all the times that the Army mis-delivered—or didn't deliver at all—this time it had supplied personnel magnificently.

There had been the bewildering moment when the tall brunette with hair falling in soft waves to her shoulder had shown up at Incirlik Air Base.

"Chief Petty Officer Teresa Mann assigned to your detail," she'd dropped a set of transit orders into his lap.

"I didn't—" *ask for a liaison officer,* he almost said, but bit off the words. There was something about how a Special Operations field soldier stood that no one else could match. It wasn't attitude, it was competence. And she had it. His initial thought was to ask her the usual litany of questions when facing an unknown soldier with undefined skills, but then he thought better of it—when the roles were reversed, those questions always just pissed him off. So instead he went with, "What was your last assignment?"

And she'd given him the blank stare of experience with those cool brown eyes that said it was classified and he needed to find himself a new question. It was a good sign that her looks aside, she was one put-together soldier. Factor those in and…he looked down at her orders quickly for a distraction. She had her Master Parachutist Badge and also had the security clearance to know what was and wasn't classified—both key elements to this operation.

Hal had waved her to a seat and started right in on the briefing. As they worked out the final shape of the plan, she'd offered suggestions that showed field experience—not deep field experience, but rough enough to learn important lessons the hard way. Maybe women making it through the Delta Selection process and OTC wasn't such an obscure possibility.

Ten thousand feet. On target.

The next bolt of lightning was so close that he wondered if they were about to be fried in the sky. Not that it would phase Petty Officer Mann. His few lame attempts at getting personal had revealed her near-robotic degree of control and dedication to the service. Gorgeous, but she had a wind chill factor even worse than the storm's.

3

Teresa figured that her oxygen reserve had run out prematurely and she was going to have to peel back her mask and risk frostbite, when it occurred to her that she wasn't breathing at all. With a sharp gasp, she sucked in oxygen, and her head cleared.

Eight thousand.

Another breath that tasted of panic. She bit it back hard and forced her next breath to be even and regulated.

That last lightning flash had been so close she could still feel the induced charge across her skin. She'd been staring into the darkness toward Hal Waldman, her brain seeking some confirmation that she wasn't alone in this madness, went the bolt had shocked through the clouds close behind her and revealed him in sharp relief against the storm. The brutal thump of thunder slammed her closer to him and momentarily drowned out both wind and storm.

Closer to him. She knew nothing about him, but he exuded confidence and safety. Even in this crazy jump, she felt as if it was possible merely because he fell alongside her.

She'd worked heavy-duty Coast Guard missions before, but when her commander had offered her a shot at jumping with the legendary Delta Force, she'd leapt at the chance. For some idiot reason she'd thought that three years in the MSST had prepared her for anything, but it certainly hadn't prepared her for this. Jumping in this weather proved that the Delta guys really were as nuts as rumor said—something she'd never quite believed until this moment.

She'd been ready for macho bravura and a dismissive attitude. What she hadn't been ready for was when Master Sergeant Hal

Waldman had simply waved her to a seat and started right into the briefing without so much as a hello. Pure soldier, a hundred-percent business. When he'd eventually offered a few openings to friendly conversation, she'd been too surprised to react before he shrugged and moved on.

Even after three years, most of the MSST cadre didn't treat her with such simple acceptance. Women were only a little more common there than they were in Special Operations—as in not at all.

Sergeant Waldman's steadiness had helped keep her own nerves calm. She'd only been assigned to carefully planned missions before, until she'd chafed at the restriction, as if she somehow wasn't good enough. Delta's specialty was the short notice plunge into unknown conditions. Someone was finally trusting her out on the edge…actually way past it. Ice fogged most of her facemask and the wind had bitten right through her flight-suit despite the waterproof materials and thick fleece lining.

Three thousand. Two. At one-five she pulled her ripcord and by one thousand, the black chute opened with a sharp crack and the harness slammed up against her crotch and tried to remove her breasts—standard fare for the ride.

A flash of lightning, more distant this time, revealed Hal Waldman close by and still no sign of the ground. She corrected right, then left to tuck in tight behind him.

The squall blowing out of the southwest at forty knots made for excellent cover, but she couldn't believe they'd actually been crazy enough to jump in it.

A parachute typically landed going under twenty miles an hour; a hard stall at the last second could cut that in half. They were going to be blown backwards while flying full-speed forward. Nothing in her combat training had prepared her for that.

A final glance at the GPS showed that Hal already had them flying into the wind and, yes, they were traveling backwards.

"This wasn't in any of my training!" she shouted at the wind.

"Mine either."

Crap!

She'd forgotten that they had an open

radio link as long as they were within fifty meters of each other.

"Not exactly a confidence builder, Waldman."

"It's the Army, what do you expect?"

She hadn't expected Master Sergeant Hal Waldman to be understanding, let alone have any hint of humor. The combination was almost enough to make her bobble the descent.

Unit operators were a tough, manly-men bunch, but with four older brothers she knew how to handle that. A Delta soldier would never admit a weakness, yet Hal had just admitted that he too was riding the hairy edge at the moment and it oddly gave her some hope.

They were below two hundred feet when they broke out of the cloud cover.

Her night-vision goggles revealed a classic upper-middle class Iraqi compound displayed in an NVG's thousand shades of green heat. A high stone wall around a dusty courtyard that was currently a muddy courtyard. Several solid-looking buildings that she hoped they didn't hit. A variety of miscellaneous obstacles.

Too late to do more than pick where they were going to crash land, she let nerves and trained reflexes take over. Rather than stalling the chute to kill forward motion, they kept moving ahead at full flight into the wind… and the wind kept carrying them backward. She had to keep glancing over her shoulder to make sure she was being blown toward a safe landing zone.

In a blur too fast for her mind to record, she adjusted to avoid a parked Toyota pickup, dodged a stone well, and slammed backward into the mud. Their chutes dragged them across the courtyard until they slammed into the perimeter wall together. Once she decided she was alive and opened her eyes, her night vision revealed two cows and a goat that were too startled to do more than stare as they cowered there seeking some protection against the wall.

She, Hal, and their chutes were all tangled together. Hal's arms were pinned to her body by a snarl of nylon paracords and his facemask was pressed hard against hers—their noses practically touching except for the two thin layers of plastic.

Hal struggled briefly but was unable to free himself. He didn't use the opportunity for a quick feel even though his arms were wrapped around her.

Thinking back she was able to reconstruct that at the last moment he'd grabbed her and taken the brunt of the slam into the wall himself in order to spare her, which was damned decent—they'd hit hard. She was winded despite the buffer.

They each managed to pull a hand free and peel off their facemasks now that they were out of oxygen. The rain, so cold and painful at altitude, was a refreshing wash across her heated face. The snarl of the paracord kept their faces only inches apart, but he eased the awkwardness with a smile and joke.

"What do you do for fun when you aren't doing crazy shit like this?"

A cow stepped closer to sniff at them as a slap of wind slammed the stink of cow breath and manure at her.

"Barbeque," she told the cow. "Four older brothers, I'm big on barbeque."

4

Hal made a quick scan of the yard as he laughed at her joke. Their arrival had gone by unobserved, which was good as they were still snarled together and he couldn't draw so much as a penknife. Her humor after so dangerous a flight helped steady him as he worked to free himself and pack his chute. And their brief entanglement that had forced him into contact with a number of parts of Petty Officer Mann's body—for which he apologized—he couldn't regret for an instant. Despite flight gear, harness, and a small field pack, it had been impossible to avoid the body he'd sat only inches from for the last twenty-seven hours.

Every curve that he'd so appreciated watching, he now knew was backed up by muscle in the best way possible.

She'd also proven to have a sharp intellect and hadn't panicked during the scariest jump *he* had ever been on. Now it was time to see if her skills played out in the field. He certainly hoped so, because they were in the deep end now. For one, he hadn't planned on landing *inside* the compound itself—if this was the right one. The houses were crowded close together here up against the city walls, the big homes of the wealthy and powerful. Here they were close enough to the country to still have ties and traditions there, like the farm animals in the courtyard.

After untangling himself, Hal was only seconds ahead of Mann on stuffing away his chute, and assembling his HK416 rifle and scope. By unspoken consent they swept the compound from opposite directions. The scopes interfaced with their NVGs and showed no guards, which was odd.

Actually, maybe it wasn't. After the

pounding they'd taken in the storm, it seemed mild here on the ground by comparison. By any other standards though it was an awful night—a mush of sleet and freezing rain thick enough to haze the main house and the guard's quarters only a hundred feet away.

His scan also proved that they were in the right place. A pre-storm drone's surveillance had matched the layout which he had memorized during planning.

Inspection complete, he chopped a hand toward the guard's quarters where a dim light showed in the window. They'd all be huddled inside, out of the storm, probably coming out only for hourly patrols.

Hal checked his watch, oh-two-fourteen. If the guards had any common sense, none of them would be any emerging for another forty-six minutes. A single light in one of the windows showed that someone was still awake.

He was ten feet from the door when it swung open.

Crap! Fifteen-minute patrols. Oh-two-fifteen. Oh-two-thirty.

Maintaining his sprint, he drove his

shoulder straight into the man's gut. With a grunt he collapsed back into the room with Hal on top of him. He brought the stock of his rifle sharply up against the man's chin who then collapsed into unconsciousness. Since the guard had stepped from the lit room into the darkness, his vision had been compromised. He wouldn't be able to report anything of what or who had hit him.

Hal crouched, tense and alert.

A single lamp. A half dozen chairs. A table with a book set face down on its surface. A door to the right and another to the left. A deafening drum roll of rain drove against the tin roof in sharp gusts.

There was a brush against his shoulder, just enough contact to tell him Teresa was rushing by him on the right side.

Hal rolled back to his feet and eased up to the left-hand door. Teresa turned off the light and the room plunged back into night-vision green.

Poised at the doors, they both pulled out dart guns.

At a shared nod they rolled through the doors simultaneously.

Hal was standing in a tiny barren room with a circular hole in the floor and a brass pot of water for rinsing one's left hand and flushing any waste down the hole. He could see the warmth of a recent handprint on the rim of the bowl and a distinct heat by the hole in the floor. He was in a typical mid-Eastern toilet.

By the time he'd re-crossed the main room and reached the other door, Teresa was already retrieving the four darts that had knocked out the other guards.

"Got the bathroom, didn't you?"

"Yeah, how did you know?"

She pointed at the two doors and said, "No immediate outbuilding equals inside toilet. You won by..." then her grin turned wicked, "...process of elimination."

He groaned.

She held up a hand and when he responded in kind she high-fived it with enthusiasm.

Absolutely his kind of woman.

5

"Now it gets interesting."

"Interesting," Teresa did her best to match the Master Sergeant's wry tone. In the last sixteen minutes, she'd: beat up on a ham-handed Air Force grunt, performed a HALO parachute jump through the heart of a squall, spent a few minutes unsnarling herself from the splendidly hard-bodied Master Sergeant—a task she'd found herself curiously reluctant to hasten—and taken down five heavily-armed house guards without having to kill any.

"Interesting" didn't begin to cover it.

This was the kind of mission she'd dreamed of for years. Military parents bred military kids and it was finally her turn. It wouldn't last. By tomorrow she could be back at MSST which was far more about training and being ready than action, but for now she'd dive in headfirst.

Again, a careful scan of the grounds from the guard-house door.

No action.

They swept across the yard to the main house.

Their target obviously wasn't a man prone to worrying. He maintained only minimal guards with only one at a time on night duty patrol. She and Hal had planned for much more security when they were designing the mission.

The front door was locked. Rather than breaching it, Hal signaled her left as he circled right. No hovering. No protecting the "fragile female." In the Master Sergeant's world you were either a soldier or you weren't. It was like a breath of fresh air. No man except her dad had ever believed in her like that.

Side of the house was clear.

At the rear, the only person Teresa encountered was Hal coming around the other way. There were two more goats sleeping in the protection of the narrow space between the stone-and-mortar house and the compound's concrete rear wall, but Hal stepped by them so carefully they barely woke. A powerful soldier who could move so lightly; he was oddly beautiful to watch—part dancer and part walking death.

There was no door, but there was a window. Locked.

Through the glass they could see the clear heat signature of a couple lying together in a bed. She and Hal shifted to another window, smaller and higher.

"I'll boost you up," Hal knelt and cupped his hands.

"No. Me." She had an idea, saw the opportunity, and didn't give him a choice. She knelt quickly with one knee in the slush and the other raised. With her boot firmly planted, her knee would make a solid step for him.

He shrugged, stepped on her knee, and balanced a moment to spread tape on the glass. He waited for a renewed blast of wind from the storm and punched it with a gloved fist—the tape prevented any shards from falling to shatter loudly on the interior floor—then he reached through and unlocked it. In moments his weight was gone.

She called up softly, "You in the shitter again?"

6

Hal sighed.

Nothing got past Teresa. Not only had he been set up, but he'd climbed right into it without thinking.

He was indeed standing in the master bathroom. A far nicer version than the one in the guard's quarters with a modern shower, a sit-down toilet, and tile work that was probably attractive but was all a uniform dark green, almost black with lack of heat in his NVGs...but still "in the shitter again."

Teresa handed through her rifle, then with a jump-and-grab, slipped through the window and landed beside him. She applied a friendly nudge in the ribs, that lost him about half his air, and then they moved forward into the house. A quick scouting revealed that it was unoccupied except for the master bedroom; they met again outside the closed bedroom door.

No noise or light within.

Hal pulled out a fiber-optic viewer and slipped it under the door. Both figures still lay on the bed, neither appeared to have moved.

At his nod, Teresa opened the door, while he remained low by the floor with his weapon raised.

One of the figures sat up, a woman with long hair and a heavy nightgown. She turned to face them. "You're early," she said in passable English. "What are you doing here?"

Hal had wanted to keep this mission as low profile as possible, so when the Air Force had a flight already planned that would only need a small route diversion, he'd taken it, adjusting the "preferred" schedule that had accompanied the mission details to match the Air Force's.

The man stirred slowly.

Hal spotted the AK-47 leaning against the wall within easy reach. He moved so that he stood between it and the man who came awake with a start. The man reached for the rifle and shouted in alarm when his hand ran into Hal's thigh in the dark.

"Who are you? What are you doing here? I am just a businessman, but I have friends." The man's voice rose until he was shouting in Arabic.

"I think," Teresa said softly over the radio, "that the man we're looking for is a woman."

The man rose and struck out at him. His fist landed squarely against the butt of Hal's Glock 17 handgun that he wore at the center of his gut for a faster draw. The man yelped as he jerked back his injured hand.

7

"Another hour," the woman insisted, "and I would have been standing out in the yard."

"We're here now," Hal snapped.

Irritation was another new emotion in Teresa's catalog of unexpected sides to Hal Waldman. Accepting a woman without question, not caught staring at her too often, a sense of humor, and now irritation—proving that he actually did have emotions. What else was hidden behind the Master Sergeant's all-business tough-guy mask?

Of course, she'd be irritated too if she'd had to subdue the man in his own bed.

Neither the gag nor having his hands and feet bound had silenced him; that had taken Hal resting the barrel of his HK416 rifle against his chest and flicking off the safety.

"What does it matter, lady? Let's get moving before your guards wake up."

Which shouldn't be for two more hours with the dose Teresa had shot into them.

The woman shifted uncomfortably.

Teresa had spent the last year in forward language support for Special Operations Forces working as trainers and advisors in Syria—one of the reasons she'd been so close to hand when the mission call came. Her best friend in high school had been from Egypt, which had influenced Teresa to learn Arabic and spend her Junior Year Abroad in Cairo. The last year in theater had polished her vocabulary and accent.

It had also taught her that many Iraqi women, no matter how Westernized, were uncomfortable talking directly to a man.

"You may speak to me," Teresa remained with English as that was the language the woman had been using.

"If you had taken me when you were

supposed to, my husband would know nothing. He would remain in his business and I would be able to deliver all of his passwords to you without him any wiser."

"Don't you think he would have guessed?"

The woman looked over at her husband in a way that required no knowledge of language to translate between two women of any culture.

Teresa glanced at Hal. He hadn't missed the look either. Every attempt she made to pigeonhole him failed miserably. Macho Delta operators weren't supposed to understand when a woman knew they were the brains behind the successful man.

"Why would we want his passwords, but not him?" Hal asked.

The woman continued to stare at Teresa as if Hal didn't exist.

Teresa wondered quite how that was possible. By the glow of the single bedside light—that faded and flickered deeply with each blast of the outside storm—Master Sergeant Hal Waldman looked every inch the conquering hero.

"Because," the woman replied softly, "his

business is communications. He designed
the secure communications system between
Taliban cells throughout the region."

8

Their exfiltration plan had included one cooperative male extractee: not a woman and a very unwilling man. Hal had been puzzling over how to adapt to that when Teresa hit the solution.

Now they were all piled in the family Toyota Highlander. The women were both in the backseat, fully covered by robe and veil. The man was in the driver's seat, convinced to behave by the HK416 pressed into his ribcage from inside Hal's own voluminous robe and veil.

"How do you see while wearing this?" The

narrow slit at his eyes, covered by a fine mesh to block any view in, might be ideal cover but every time he moved his head what little view he had disappeared behind some fold of fabric.

"Careful," Teresa warned him, "or we'll make you wear nylons for a day. And don't think I can't make you do it."

There wasn't a chance she'd succeed, but he'd wager it would be fun if she tried.

The other woman laughed aloud, then the sound was suddenly muffled as they rounded a corner and pulled up to a military checkpoint.

With a careful prod of the HK, the man behaved.

To Hal's ear he didn't have the proper amount of complaint in his tone for being on the road at three in the morning to drive his wife and sisters to aid a sick aunt in the next town over.

Teresa leaned forward and whispered something in the man's ear. His voice faltered, then he found his stride and they were soon pulling away from the checkpoint. Soon, they were rolling down an empty stretch of highway.

Hal pulled out a satellite phone and dialed the number he'd been given. Twenty minutes later there was a roar close overhead as if the storm, which had been abating, was now hammering back down on them.

Then in the headlights, he could pick out an all-black Night Stalkers Chinook helicopter landing in the middle of the road with its rear ramp down.

They drove straight aboard. After some jockeying, the Loadmaster signaled for lockdown and they were tied into place. They were aloft within two minutes of the helicopter's arrival.

"Let's switch seats and I'll tie him back up."

"Oh, he'll behave," Teresa said with utter confidence.

"What makes you say that?"

"I told him what I'd do to his manhood with my knife if he didn't do everything perfectly. I gave him every reason to believe me."

Even if the man didn't speak any English, he was glancing over at Hal nervously as if guessing the conversation and seeking protection.

Hal grimaced in sympathetic pain. "Maybe I won't take your nylons bet."

"Pity," a woman's voice spoke from close beside him. The Loadmaster—a woman—was leaning against his lowered window. "I bet you'd look cute in them."

She walked away, humming the tune to a Gypsy Rose Lee stripper song.

"Not a chance," he called out after her, but she just broke into song. Strangely enough the other members of the Chinook's crew joined in as they banked hard, racing back toward friendly territory.

He turned back to face Teresa in the backseat, "Not a chance."

But he sure wouldn't mind seeing Chief Petty Officer Teresa Mann in a pair—a flawless soldier with an amazing body. That was a deadly combo indeed.

9

Hal didn't see anything of Teresa Mann after their first few minutes back on the ground. By the time he'd gone through debrief and delivered his two charges, she had faded into the dawn and was already gone back into whatever invisible Coast Guard fog bank she'd popped out of.

Searching for her hadn't helped, not that his operational tempo allowed much time to do so.

An inquiry to MSST was returned with a: *The United States Coast Guard does not respond to requests for information about the Maritime Safety and Security Team.*

A follow-up to the USCG itself simply addressed to CPO Teresa Mann was returned with the puzzling endorsement: *No longer with the service.*

A Google search returned 23,880 hits, and none of them were her as far as he could tell—except for a seriously cute high school yearbook photo from some unpronounceable high school in Poughkeepsie, New York.

Pounding his head against the wall hadn't helped either.

By mid-summer he'd decided that he would give it one more shot. He'd been rotated back to Fort Bragg, North Carolina for some Unit refresher training. He didn't even know where to begin to look for her now that he was stateside, but there had to be some lead he could pick up. If not, he promised himself he'd stop being pitiful about a woman he'd known barely thirty-six hours six months ago…and he'd do that very soon.

The squad he'd spent a long day simulating room-clearing with dragged him out on the town. Hal wasn't really in the mood for some dive bar, but you just didn't turn down seven other grunts who'd fired a thousand rounds each together.

They were three bars into Bragg Boulevard before he gave in and just went with the flow. Tomorrow was a "dark" day— an actual, honest-to-god, stateside day of rest. By the fifth bar they were down to three others plus himself. The other four had been peeled off by some of the bar bait with long legs and bottle-blond hair that always flowed around Fort Bragg.

At the seventh bar, he ended up alone. Hal kind of remembered the other three saying they were moving on, but he'd ground to a halt here. He wasn't drunk, hadn't finished a whole beer in any of the places, but he was slowing down.

An hour later and half a beer in, he wondered if this was where he'd be sleeping tonight. It was a good spot: back in the corner, a band that was just loud enough to turn his brain into tapioca pudding without beating him to death, and a pleasant enough flow of female scenery to keep him entertained. None of them really grabbed his attention but they were fun to watch. And none bothered to gun for the solitary drinker in the corner. When on assignment he usually slept in far worse places.

He knew how he must look. The slight shell-shock of someone fresh back from the front suddenly surrounded by the bounties of America. Unless they were one of your buddies, you just left guys like him alone until they were back up to speed.

The room shifted.

The noise level didn't change.

But there had been something. It was the sort of thing that only a trained operator would probably notice; the *feel* had altered.

He started hunting for the source and it didn't take long to spot. Nine new arrivals— soldiers who moved like operators. But it wasn't just that they were Special Ops; you couldn't get a drink within fifty miles of Fort Bragg without running into some form of top soldier.

Hal blinked a couple of times to bring them into sharper focus.

It wasn't just that they were Delta, though they were unquestionably from The Unit.

There was also a strange energy about

them, as if every step they took was suddenly their first.

A new class had graduated from the Operator's Training Course. Nobody else moved that way; that impossible bravado generated by finally knowing that for a fact, you are one of the very best warriors on the planet. There was an electrical charge that sizzled off their every step.

He should go over and buy them a round, but he hated giving up his corner table.

He should…

A tenth soldier walked in, moving with that same impossible confidence.

The only woman among them, he'd know her anywhere even though her hair was shorter, because only one woman possessed the finest ass in the military.

And when she turned and spotted him? That smile lit him up like one of those lightning bolts had finally caught him.

That's why she'd disappeared off the grid and out of MSST; she'd gone for Delta Selection and made it through the six months of OTC.

He could feel the smile on his own face.

Unit Operator Teresa Mann looked as if she too had been struck by lightning and it looked damn good on her.

About the Author

M. L. Buchman has over 40 novels in print. His military romantic suspense books have been named Barnes & Noble and NPR "Top 5 of the year" and *Booklist* "Top 10 of the Year." He has been nominated for the Reviewer's Choice Award for "Top 10 Romantic Suspense of 2014" by *RT Book Reviews.* In addition to romance, he also writes thrillers, fantasy, and science fiction.

In among his career as a corporate project manager he has: rebuilt and single-handed a fifty-foot sailboat, both flown and jumped out of airplanes, designed and built two houses, and bicycled solo around the world.

He is now making his living as a full-time writer on the Oregon Coast with his beloved wife. He is constantly amazed at what you can do with a degree in Geophysics. You may keep up with his writing by subscribing to his newsletter at www.mlbuchman.com.

Target Engaged (excerpt)
-a Delta Force novel-

Carla Anderson rolled up to the looming, storm-fence gate on her brother's midnight-blue Kawasaki Ninja 1000 motorcycle. The pounding of the engine against her sore butt emphasized every mile from Fort Carson in Pueblo, Colorado, home of the 4th Infantry and hopefully never again the home of

Sergeant Carla Anderson. The bike was all she had left of Clay, other than a folded flag, and she was here to honor that.

If this was the correct "here."

A small guard post stood by the gate into a broad, dusty compound. It looked deserted and she didn't see even a camera.

This *was* Fort Bragg, North Carolina. She knew that much. Two hundred and fifty square miles of military installation, not counting the addition of the neighboring Pope Army Airfield.

She'd gotten her Airborne parachute training here and had never even known what was hidden in this remote corner. Bragg was exactly the sort of place where a tiny, elite unit of the U.S. military could disappear—in plain sight.

This back corner of the home of the 82nd Airborne was harder to find than it looked. What she could see of the compound through the fence definitely ranked "worst on base."

The setup was totally whacked.

Standing outside the fence at the guard post she could see a large, squat building across the compound. The gray concrete building was incongruously cheerful with bright pink roses along the front walkway— the only landscaping visible anywhere. More recent buildings—in better condition only because they were newer—ranged off to the right. She could breach the old fence in a dozen different places just in the hundred-yard span she could see before it disappeared into a clump of scrub and low trees drooping in the June heat.

Wholly indefensible.

There was no way that this could be the headquarters of the top combat unit in any country's military.

Unless this really was their home, in which case the indefensible fence—in-defence-ible?— was a complete sham designed to fool a sucker. She'd stick with the main gate.

She peeled off her helmet and scrubbed at her long brown hair to get some air back into her scalp. Guys always went gaga over her hair, which was a useful distraction at times. She always wore it as long as her successive commanders allowed. Pushing the limits was one of her personal life policies.

She couldn't help herself. When there was

a limit, Carla always had to see just how far it could be nudged. Surprisingly far was usually the answer. Her hair had been at earlobe length in Basic. By the time she joined her first forward combat team, it brushed her jaw. Now it was down on her shoulders. It was actually something of a pain in the ass at this length—another couple inches before it could reliably ponytail—but she did like having the longest hair in the entire unit.

Carla called out a loud "Hello!" at the empty compound shimmering in the heat haze.

No response.

Using her boot in case the tall chain-link fence was electrified, she gave it a hard shake, making it rattle loudly in the dead air. Not even any birdsong in the oppressive midday heat.

A rangy man in his late forties or early fifties, his hair half gone to gray, wandered around from behind a small shack as if he just happened to be there by chance. He was dressed like any off-duty soldier: worn khaki pants, a black T-shirt, and scuffed Army boots. He slouched to a stop and tipped his head to study her from behind his Ray-Bans. He needed a haircut and a shave. This was not a soldier out to make a good first impression.

"Don't y'all get hot in that gear?" He nodded to indicate her riding leathers without raking his eyes down her frame, which was both unusual and appreciated.

"Only on warm days," she answered him. It was June in North Carolina. The temperature had crossed ninety hours ago and the air was humid enough to swim in, but complaining never got you anywhere.

"What do you need?"

So much for the pleasantries. "Looking for Delta."

"Never heard of it," the man replied with a negligent shrug. But something about how he did it told her she was in the right place.

"Combat Applications Group?" Delta Force had many names, and they certainly lived to "apply combat" to a situation. No one on the planet did it better.

His next shrug was eloquent.

Delta Lesson One: *Folks on the inside of the wire didn't call it Delta Force. It was CAG or "The Unit."* She got it. Check. Still easier to think of it as Delta though.

She pulled out her orders and held them up. "Received a set of these. Says to show up here today."

"Let me see that."

"Let me through the gate and you can look at it as long as you want."

"Sass!" He made it an accusation.

"Nope. Just don't want them getting damaged or lost maybe by accident." She offered her blandest smile with that.

"They're that important to you, girlie?"

"Yep!"

He cracked what might have been the start of a grin, but it didn't get far on that grim face. Then he opened the gate and she idled the bike forward, scuffing her boots through the dust.

From this side she could see that the chain link was wholly intact. There was a five-meter swath of scorched earth inside the fence line. Through the heat haze, she could see both infrared and laser spy eyes down the length of the wire. And that was only the defenses she could see. So…a very not inde-fence-ible fence.

Absolutely the right place.

When she went to hold out the orders, he waved them aside.

"Don't you want to see them?" This had to be the right place. She was the first woman in history to walk through The Unit's gates by order. A part of her wanted the man to acknowledge that. Any man. A Marine Corps marching band wouldn't have been out of order.

She wanted to stand again as she had on that very first day, raising her right hand. "I, Carla Anderson, do solemnly swear that I will support and defend the Constitution…"

She shoved that aside. The only man's acknowledgment she'd ever cared about was her big brother's, and he was gone.

The man just turned away and spoke to her over his shoulder as he closed the gate behind her bike. "Go ahead and check in. You're one of the last to arrive. We start in a couple hours"—as if it were a blasted dinner party. "And I already saw those orders when I signed them. Now put them away before someone else sees them and thinks you're still a soldier." He walked away.

She watched the man's retreating back. *He'd* signed her orders?

That was the notoriously hard-ass Colonel Charlie Brighton?

What the hell was the leader of the U.S. Army's Tier One asset doing manning the gate? Duh…assessing new applicants.

This place *was* whacked. Totally!

There were only three Tier One assets in the entire U.S. military. There was Navy's Special Warfare Development Group, DEVGRU, that the public thought was called SEAL Team Six—although it hadn't been named that for thirty years now. There was the Air Force's 24th STS—which pretty much no one on the outside had ever heard of. And there was the 1st Special Forces Operational Detachment—Delta—whose very existence was still denied by the Pentagon despite four decades of operations, several books, and a couple of seriously off-the-mark movies that were still fun to watch because Chuck Norris kicked ass even under the stupidest of circumstances.

Total Tier One women across all three teams? Zero.

About to be? One. Staff Sergeant First Class Carla Anderson.

Where did she need to go to check in? There was no signage. No drill sergeant hovering. No—

Delta Lesson Number Two: *You aren't in the Army anymore, sister.*

No longer a soldier, as the Colonel had said, at least not while on The Unit's side of the fence. On this side they weren't regular Army; they were "other."

If that meant she had to take care of herself, well, that was a lesson she'd learned long ago. Against stereotype, her well-bred, East Coast white-guy dad was the drunk. Her dirt-poor half Tennessee Cherokee, half Colorado settler mom, who'd passed her dusky skin and dark hair on to her daughter, had been a sober and serious woman. She'd also been a casualty of an Afghanistan dust-bowl IED while serving in the National Guard. Carla's big brother Clay now lay beside Mom in Arlington National Cemetery. Dead from a training accident. Except your average training accident didn't include a posthumous rank bump, a medal, and coming home in a sealed box reportedly with no face.

Clay had flown helicopters in the Army's 160th SOAR with the famous Majors Beale and Henderson. Well, famous in the world of people who'd flown with the Special Operations Aviation Regiment, or their little sisters who'd begged for stories of them whenever big brothers were home on leave. Otherwise totally invisible.

Clay had clearly died on a black op that she'd never be told a word of, so she didn't bother asking. Which was okay. He knew the risks, just as Mom had. Just as she herself had when she'd signed up the day of Clay's funeral, four years ago. She'd been on the front lines ever since and so far lived to tell about it.

Carla popped Clay's Ninja—which is how she still thought of it, even after riding it for four years—back into first and rolled it slowly up to the building with the pink roses. As good a place to start as any.

***

"Hey, check out this shit!"
Sergeant First Class Kyle Reeves looked out

the window of the mess hall at the guy's call. Sergeant Ralph last-name-already-forgotten was 75th Rangers and too damn proud of it.

Though…damn! Ralphie was onto something.

Kyle would definitely check out *this shit.*

Babe on a hot bike, looking like she knew how to handle it.

Through the window, he inspected her lean length as she clambered off the machine. Army boots. So call her five-eight, a hundred and thirty, and every part that wasn't amazing curves looked like serious muscle. Hair the color of lush, dark caramel brushed her shoulders but moved like the finest silk, her skin permanently the color of the darkest tan. Women in magazines didn't look that hot. Those women always looked anorexic to him anyway, even the pinup babes displayed on Hesco barriers at forward operating bases up in the Hindu Kush where he'd done too much of the last couple years.

This woman didn't look like that for a second. She looked powerful. And dangerous.

Her tight leathers revealed muscles made of pure soldier.

Ralph Something moseyed out of the mess-hall building where the hundred selectees were hanging out to await the start of the next testing class at sundown.

Well, Kyle sure wasn't going to pass up the opportunity for a closer look. Though seeing Ralph's attitude, Kyle hung back a bit so that he wouldn't be too closely associated with the dickhead.

Ralph had been spoiling for a fight ever since he'd found out he was one of the least experienced guys to show up for Delta selection. He was from the 75th Ranger Regiment, but his deployments hadn't seen much action. Each of his attempts to brag for status had gotten him absolutely nowhere.

Most of the guys here were 75th Rangers, 82nd Airborne, or Green Beret Special Forces like himself. And most had seen a shitload of action because that was the nature of the world at the moment. There were a couple SEALs who hadn't made SEAL Team Six and probably weren't going to make Delta, a dude from the Secret Service Hostage Rescue Team who wasn't going to last a day no matter how good a shot he was, and two guys who were regular Army.

The question of the moment though, who was she?

Her biking leathers were high-end, sewn in a jagged lightning-bolt pattern of yellow on smoke gray. It made her look like she was racing at full tilt while standing still. He imagined her hunched over her midnight-blue machine and hustling down the road at her Ninja's top speed—which was north of 150. He definitely had to see that one day.

Kyle blessed the inspiration on his last leave that had made him walk past the small Toyota pickup that had looked so practical and buy the wildfire-red Ducati Multistrada 1200 instead. Pity his bike was parked around the back of the barracks at the moment. Maybe they could do a little bonding over their rides. Her machine looked absolutely cherry.

Much like its rider.

Ralph walked right up to her with all his arrogant and stupid hanging out for everyone to see. The other soldiers began filtering outside to watch the show.

"Well, girlie, looks like you pulled into the wrong spot. This here is Delta territory."

Kyle thought about stopping Ralph, thought that someone should give the guy a good beating, but Dad had taught him control. He would take Ralph down if he got aggressive, but he really didn't want to be associated with the jerk, even by grabbing him back.

The woman turned to face them, then unzipped the front of her jacket in one of those long, slow movie moves. The sunlight shimmered across her hair as she gave it an "unthinking" toss. Wraparound dark glasses hid her eyes, adding to the mystery.

He could see what there was of Ralph's brain imploding from lack of blood. He felt the effect himself despite standing a half-dozen paces farther back.

She wasn't hot; she sizzled. Her parting leathers revealed an Army green T-shirt and proof that the very nice contours suggested by her outer gear were completely genuine. Her curves weren't big—she had a lean build—but they were as pure woman as her shoulders and legs were pure soldier.

"There's a man who called me 'girlie' earlier." Her voice was smooth and seductive, not low and throaty, but rich and filled with nuance.

She sounded like one of those people who could hypnotize a Cobra, either the snake or the attack helicopter.

"*He's* a bird colonel. He can call me that if he wants. *You* aren't nothing but meat walking on sacred ground and wishing he belonged."

Kyle nodded to himself. The "girlie" got it in one.

"*You*"—she jabbed a finger into Sergeant Ralph Something's chest—"do not get 'girlie' privileges. *We* clear?"

"Oh, sweetheart, I can think of plenty of privileges that you'll want to be giving to—" His hand only made it halfway to stroking her hair.

If Kyle hadn't been Green Beret trained, he wouldn't have seen it because she moved so fast and clean.

"—*me!*" Ralph's voice shot upward on a sharp squeak.

The woman had Ralph's pinkie bent to

the edge of dislocation and, before the man could react, had leveraged it behind his back and upward until old Ralph Something was perched on his toes trying to ease the pressure. With her free hand, she shoved against the middle of his back to send him stumbling out of control into the concrete wall of the mess hall with a loud *clonk* when his head hit.

Minimum force, maximum result. The Unit's way.

She eased off on his finger and old Ralph dropped to the dirt like a sack of potatoes. He didn't move much.

"Oops." She turned to face the crowd that had gathered.

She didn't even have to say, "Anyone else?" Her look said plenty.

Kyle began to applaud. He wasn't the only one, but he was in the minority. Most of the guys were doing a wait and see.

A couple looked pissed.

Everyone knew that the Marines' combat training had graduated a few women, but that was just jarheads on the ground.

This was Delta. The Unit was Tier One. A Special Mission Unit. They were supposed to be the one true bastion of male dominance. No one had warned them that a woman was coming in.

Just one woman, Kyle thought. The first one. How exceptional did that make her? Pretty damn was his guess. Even if she didn't last the first day, still pretty damn. And damn pretty. He'd bet on dark eyes behind her wraparound shades. She didn't take them off, so it was a bet he'd have to settle later on.

A couple corpsmen came over and carted Ralph Something away even though he was already sitting up—just dazed with a bloody cut on his forehead.

The Deltas who'd come out to watch the show from a few buildings down didn't say a word before going back to whatever they'd been doing.

Kyle made a bet with himself that Ralph Something wouldn't be showing up at sundown's first roll call. They'd just lost the first one of the class and the selection process hadn't even begun. Or maybe it just had.

"Where's check-in?" Her voice really was as lush as her hair, and it took Kyle a moment to focus on the actual words.

He pointed at the next building over and received a nod of thanks.

That made watching her walk away in those tight leathers strictly a bonus.

Available at fine retailers everywhere

Visit www.mlbuchman.com for more details

Other works by M.L. Buchman

Angelo's Hearth
Where Dreams are Born
Where Dreams Reside
Maria's Christmas Table
Where Dreams Unfold
Where Dreams Are Written

Dieties Anonymous
Cookbook from Hell: Reheated
Saviors 101

Thrillers
Swap Out!
One Chef!
Two Chef!

SF/F Titles
Nara
Monk's Maze

CPSIA information can be obtained at www.ICGtesting.com
Printed in the USA
LVOW11s1612010316

477309LV00001B/13/P